Junior Great Books

SERIES 2 · BOOK TWO

BEING YOURSELF

JUNIOR GREAT BOOKS®

SERIES 2 · BOOK TWO   BEING YOURSELF

The Great Books Foundation
A nonprofit educational organization

Copyright © 2015 by The Great Books Foundation
Chicago, Illinois
All rights reserved
ISBN 978-1-939014-88-7

2   4   6   8   9   7   5   3   1
Printed in the United States of America

Published and distributed by

THE GREAT BOOKS FOUNDATION
A nonprofit educational organization

35 East Wacker Drive, Suite 400

Chicago, IL 60601

www.greatbooks.org

CONTENTS

INTRODUCTION

Welcome to Book Two of Junior Great Books!
Here are some things to remember as you read
and talk about the stories in this book.

You will begin by listening to the story
and thinking of questions about it. Then your
teacher will ask you to share your questions
with everyone. Remember that any question
you have about the story is worth asking.

The teacher will write down all questions so everyone can help think about them.

Some questions can be answered right away. Others will be saved to talk or write about later.

Before the discussion, you will get to hear the story again, and do activities and answer questions that help you think more about it.

When it is time for the discussion, you will sit in a circle or square so everyone can see and hear one another. Your teacher will then ask a question about what the story means. This **interpretive question** will have more than one good answer. The teacher will ask all of you to say more about your ideas and find evidence for them in the story.

Your teacher will not ask for the "right" answer to the discussion question—there will be many good answers. At the end of the discussion everyone will understand the story better, even if you have different ideas about it. This kind of discussion is called a **Shared Inquiry™ discussion.**

Dos and Don'ts in Discussion

DO

Let other people talk, and listen to what they say.

DON'T

Talk while other people are talking.

DO

Share your ideas about the story. You may have an idea no one else has thought of.

DON'T

Be afraid to say what you're thinking about the story.

DO

Be polite when
you disagree
with someone.

DON'T

Get angry when
someone disagrees
with you.

DO

Pay attention to
the person who
is talking.

DON'T

Do things that make
it hard for people
to pay attention.

Shared Inquiry Discussion Guidelines

Following these guidelines in Shared Inquiry discussion will help everyone share ideas about the story and learn from one another.

1 Listen to or read the story twice before the discussion.

2 Discuss only the story that everyone has read.

3 Support your ideas with evidence from the story.

4 Listen to other people's ideas. You may agree or disagree with someone's answer, or ask a question about it.

5 Expect the teacher to only ask questions.

Theme Introduction

BEING YOURSELF

In this book, you will read about characters who explore what it means to "be themselves." Thinking about these stories, and about what makes you special, will give you new ideas about what it means to be yourself.

IMPORTANT QUESTIONS TO THINK ABOUT

Before starting this book, think about what it means to be yourself:

• What are some words you would use to describe yourself?

• In what ways are you like other people you know? In what ways are you different?

While you are reading the stories in this book, you might also think about this **theme question** about being yourself:

What makes it easy or hard for people to be themselves?

After reading each story, you might ask yourself the theme question again and find that you have some new ideas about it.

Once upon a time there was a little frog.

The Wise Little Toad

Rosario Ferré

Once upon a time there was a little
frog who lived on a riverbank. She
loved to bathe in its waterfalls, though
she was careful not to get in above her
waist because she was afraid to swim
underwater. At one end of that stretch
of river, the current changed course and
flowed into a pool, in the middle of which
was a big moss-covered rock where the
little frog was fond of sunning herself. At
such times her delicate nostrils opened
wide, her belly puffed up with bliss,
and her whole body palpitated like an

enormous green heart atop the rock. One
day as she was drowsing there, gulping
down a fly every so often, she heard a
little voice that said:

"Ah, little frog, little frog! How ugly you
are. Aren't you ashamed to roam about
the world with those big bulging eyes,
that monstrous head, and those croaking

sounds that you make as you sing alongside the stream? What's more, you're never going to catch up with me because you can't swim underwater."

The little frog roused herself a bit and, looking carefully about, saw a silvery little fish poking his head mockingly out of the pool. When he saw that she had spied him, the little fish gave a flick of his tail and swam off, saying:

The frog bathes in the river.
The fish sings to her and dances for her.
But the frog can't swim underwater.

Determined to overtake the little fish, the frog gathered up her courage, took a tremendous leap, and landed in the bottom of the pool. Once there, she opened her eyes very wide, but all she saw were algae, a pink shrimp, and a very old, yellow crab crawling along the bottom. She remained motionless for a number of minutes, which seemed to her

an eternity, not daring to breathe. At last
she caught sight of the silvery reflection
of the little fish in the distance, but when
she tried to catch up with him, she felt as
though her chest were being squeezed by
a steel tourniquet, and with a tremendous
leap, she rose to the surface for air.

The little frog went back to her green
rock feeling very sad and sat down there
in a thoughtful mood. For several days
she was obliged to resign herself to
putting up with the little fish's jeering as
he kept making fun of her:

> *The frog bathes in the river.*
> *Laughing, the fish dodges her.*
> *But the frog can't swim underwater.*

Finally the frog tired of this and went to
visit the Great Frog. When she saw the old
wise frog, the little frog said, "Mama Frog,
just imagine what has happened to me.
The little fish has dared me to catch up
with him, and I don't know how to swim
underwater."

15

The Great Frog affectionately stroked the little frog's head and replied, "Don't complain, my child. Nature knows why it makes the creatures of this world so different from one another." And following the advice of the Great Frog, the little frog decided to forget the matter and went far away from that pool in which she had been so unhappy.

A month went by, and a terrible drought scourged the land. The river's current lessened to the point that it turned into a small stream, then became a mere creek, and finally all that was left of it was a thin trickle. The little frog was happy once again. Since she could no longer bathe in the waterfalls because they had dried up, she leapt from stone to stone along the river's edge, bathing here and there in the water that still remained.

One day she passed by the pool with the green rock, where in bygone days she had been in the habit of sunning herself, and noted that the pool had become so much smaller that all that was left of it was a little puddle the size of an umbrella. The little frog sat down once again on her rock of the days of yore and began reflecting on the nature of life, but since it was very sunny, she soon fell asleep.

"Ah, little frog, little frog! How pretty you are! Doesn't it please you to roam about the world with those eyes that are so big, with that elegant head, and that lovely croaking song that you sing in the wildwood? If you lean forward a little, I'll let you catch me, and I'll climb up on your back so that you can get me out of here."

The little frog recognized that voice immediately, but as she was now a wise frog, she answered, "Little fish, little fish!

I may be ugly or pretty, but that no longer matters because now you're the one who can't catch me. The water is almost all dried up and you're afraid because you can hardly breathe!" And with one great leap, the little frog took off from there.

A few days later she again passed by the spot and noted that the pool had become so small that it was no larger than a bowl of soup. She then sat down on her rock once again, and soon fell asleep. A short while later she heard a feeble little voice that said, "Ah, little frog, little frog! How pretty you are! Doesn't it please you to roam about the world with those bright little eyes, with that head like a tiger's, and that lovely croaking song that you sing in the wildwood? If you lean a little way over the water, I'll climb up on your back so that you can get me out of here."

But since the little frog paid no attention to him, and didn't even open her eyes to see who it was, he plunged back down into the water.

The following day the little green frog
went back to the pool and saw that all
that was left of it now was a tiny puddle
the size of a little cup of coffee. The
silvery fish was lying on the mud, with
his tail out of the water and only his head
submerged. This time he said nothing,
and when he saw the frog take her usual
place atop the rock, he remained silent.

The little frog sat there looking at the
little fish until at last she took pity on him.

"May this be a lesson to you, little fish. Nature knows what she's doing when she makes all of us such different creatures!" And leaning over the puddle, she hoisted the little fish up onto her back and took him a long way away from there, to another pool in which there was more water.

Kevin Spoon was a lucky kid.

Doodle Flute

Daniel Pinkwater

Kevin Spoon had a nice life.

He had nice parents.

He had a nice house.

He had his own room.

He had his own bathroom.

He had his own TV.

He had his own VCR.

He had his own stereo.

He had his own computer.

He had a ten-speed bike.

He had professional running shoes.

He had a professional first baseman's glove.

He had purebred guppies.

He had a waterproof watch.

His clothes were nice.

He had pizza every day.

Kevin Spoon was a lucky kid.

His mother and father said so.

And he thought so.

In back of Kevin Spoon's house was the yard.

In the yard was the pool.

Behind the pool was the fence.

Beyond the fence was the alley.

One day, Kevin Spoon was sitting on the fence.

Someone came down the alley.

It was Mason Mintz.

A weird kid.

Mason Mintz lived up the street.

He always looked sloppy.

He wore cheap sneakers.

He had a plaid hat.

He always wore it.

Mason Mintz and his mother and father planted stuff in their back yard.

They grew pumpkins.

Mason Mintz saw Kevin Spoon.

"Ho, Kevin," he said.

"What do you mean, 'Ho,'?"
Kevin Spoon said. "You're supposed to
say 'Hi.'"

"Why?" Mason Mintz asked.

"Because that's what you say," Kevin
Spoon said. "Nobody says, 'Ho.'"

"I say it," Mason Mintz said.

"Why?"

"I like the way it sounds," Mason
Mintz said.

"You're not normal," Kevin Spoon said.

"Maybe not," Mason Mintz said. "Do
you want to see my doodle flute?"

"What is that?" Kevin Spoon asked.

"It is this," Mason Mintz said. He took something out of his back pocket.

It looked dumb.

"It looks dumb," Kevin Spoon said.

"Listen to this," Mason Mintz said.

He blew into the lumpy thing and wiggled his fingers.

It made music.

It was not like any music Kevin Spoon had ever heard.

"That's neat," he said.

"See?" Mason Mintz said.

"Where did you get that?" Kevin Spoon asked.

"It's old," Mason Mintz said. "They don't have them anymore. My father had it. He gave it to me."

"What is it called?"

"I told you. Doodle flute."

"Play it some more," Kevin Spoon said.

Mason Mintz played the doodle flute some more.

"I want to get one of those," Kevin Spoon said.

"Can't," Mason Mintz said. "This is the last one there is."

Mason Mintz went away, playing his doodle flute.

The next day, Kevin Spoon saw Mason Mintz.

"Do you still have that doodle flute?"

"Yep."

"Want to sell it?"

"Nope."

"Will you sell it to me for five dollars?"

"Nope."

"Why not?"

"Don't want to."

"I'll give you ten dollars for it," Kevin Spoon said.

"No thanks," Mason Mintz said.

"Hey! You want my waterproof watch?"
Kevin Spoon asked Mason Mintz.

"For free?" Mason Mintz asked.

"For the doodle flute," Kevin Spoon
said.

"Nope," Mason Mintz said.

"How about my running shoes?"

"Sorry."

"My running shoes *and* my waterproof
watch?"

"No can do."

"You want my guppies?"

"No."

"My stereo?"

"No."

"*All* my stuff?"

"Nix."

"Why not?
Why don't you?
Why don't you
want all my stuff?"
Kevin Spoon asked.

"I just don't,"
Mason Mintz said.

And he went away, playing his doodle flute, wearing his plaid hat.

Kevin Spoon told his parents, "I want a doodle flute."

"A flute?"

"A doodle flute."

After they had their pizza, Kevin went with his father.

They went to the music store.

"Do you have a doodle flute?" Kevin asked the man in the store.

"We have flutes, but no doodle flutes."

"How about a guitar?" Kevin's father asked.

"I want a doodle flute," Kevin said.

"Here's an electronic keyboard," Kevin's father said. "You want this?"

"I want a doodle flute," Kevin said.

"A piano?"

"No."

"A horn?"

"No."

"A harp?"

"No."

"Drums?"

"No."

"Whistles, fiddles, clarinets?"

"No."

"Anything at all?"

"No. I want a doodle flute."

Kevin and his father drove home.

"They didn't have a doodle flute,"
Kevin told his mother.

The next day, Mason Mintz came down
the alley.

"I want your doodle flute," Kevin
Spoon said.

"I know you do," Mason Mintz said.

"I offered you all my stuff for it."

"You did."

"But you won't trade."

"I won't."

"And you won't sell it for money."

"That's right."

"If I asked you to give it to me, would you?"

"Ask me and see."

"Mason Mintz, will you give me the doodle flute?"

"Yes."

"You will?"

"Sure."

Mason Mintz gave Kevin Spoon the doodle flute.

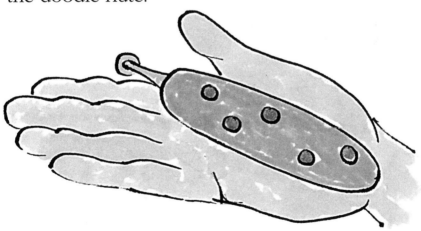

"I don't understand," Kevin Spoon said.

"What don't you understand?" Mason Mintz asked.

"Why are you giving me this? You wouldn't trade for all my stuff."

"That's just the kind of guy I am," Mason Mintz said, and walked away up the alley, wearing his plaid hat.

Kevin Spoon blew into the doodle flute. It sounded lousy.

"Rats!" Kevin Spoon said.

"I don't know how to play this."

He walked up the alley to Mason
Mintz's house.

Mason Mintz was in the back yard.

He was watering the pumpkins.

"Hey!" Kevin Spoon said.

"Ho!" Mason Mintz said.

"Teach me to play this thing."

"I can't do that," Mason Mintz said.

"Why not?" Kevin Spoon asked.

"I have given up playing the doodle
flute."

"Why? Why have you given up playing
the doodle flute?"

"Because I don't own one," Mason Mintz said. "What's the point of being a doodle flute player if you haven't got a doodle flute?"

"But I have one," Kevin Spoon said.

"Yes, you have," Mason Mintz said.

"But I can't play it," Kevin Spoon said.

"No, you can't," Mason Mintz said.

"And you won't teach me," Kevin Spoon said.

"Sorry," Mason Mintz said. "That's just the kind of guy I am."

Kevin Spoon thought.

"If you had a doodle flute," Kevin Spoon said, "and I had a doodle flute, would you teach me then?"

"Yes."

"Well then," Kevin Spoon said, "what if we *both* owned the doodle flute? What if we shared it? Would you teach me to play it?"

"That would be okay," Mason Mintz said.

So Kevin Spoon sat down with Mason Mintz in his pumpkin patch, and Mason Mintz taught Kevin Spoon to play the doodle flute.

The Rabbit was quite the best of all.

THE VELVETEEN RABBIT

Margery Williams

There was once a velveteen rabbit, and in the beginning he was really splendid. He was fat and bunchy, as a rabbit should be; his coat was spotted brown and white, he had real thread whiskers, and his ears were lined with pink sateen. On Christmas morning, when he sat wedged in the top of the Boy's stocking, with a sprig of holly between his paws, the effect was charming.

There were other things in the stocking, nuts and oranges and a toy engine, and chocolate almonds and a clockwork

mouse, but the Rabbit was quite the best
of all. For at least two hours the Boy loved
him, and then Aunts and Uncles came to
dinner, and there was a great rustling of
tissue paper and unwrapping of parcels,
and in the excitement of looking at all the
new presents the Velveteen Rabbit was
forgotten.

For a long time he lived in the toy
cupboard or on the nursery floor, and
no one thought very much about him.
He was naturally shy, and being only
made of velveteen, some of the more
expensive toys quite snubbed him. The
mechanical toys were very superior, and
looked down upon everyone else; they
were full of modern ideas, and pretended
they were real. The model boat, who
had lived through two seasons and lost
most of his paint, caught the tone from
them and never missed an opportunity of
referring to his rigging in technical terms.
The Rabbit could not claim to be a model
of anything, for he didn't know that real

rabbits existed; he thought they were all
stuffed with sawdust like himself, and he
understood that sawdust was quite out-
of-date and should never be mentioned
in modern circles. Even Timothy, the
jointed wooden lion, who was made by
the disabled soldiers and should have had
broader views, put on airs and pretended
he was connected with Government.

Between them all the poor little Rabbit
was made to feel himself very insignificant
and commonplace, and the only person
who was kind to him at all was the
Skin Horse.

The Skin Horse had lived longer in
the nursery than any of the others. He
was so old that his brown coat was
bald in patches and showed the seams
underncath, and most of the hairs in his
tail had been pulled out to string bead
necklaces. He was wise, for he had seen a
long succession of mechanical toys arrive
to boast and swagger, and by-and-by
break their mainsprings and pass away,
and he knew that they were only toys
and would never turn into anything else.
For nursery magic is very strange and
wonderful, and only those playthings that
are old and wise and experienced like the
Skin Horse understand all about it.

"What is REAL?" asked the Rabbit one
day, when they were lying side by side
near the nursery fender, before Nana
came to tidy the room. "Does it mean
having things that buzz inside you and a
stick-out handle?"

"Real isn't how you are made," said
the Skin Horse. "It's a thing that happens

to you. When a child loves you for a
long, long time, not just to play with, but
REALLY loves you, then you become
Real."

"Does it hurt?" asked the Rabbit.

"Sometimes," said the Skin Horse, for he
was always truthful. "When you are Real
you don't mind being hurt."

"Does it happen all at once, like being
wound up," he asked, "or bit by bit?"

"It doesn't happen all at once," said the
Skin Horse. "You become. It takes a long
time. That's why it doesn't often happen
to people who break easily, or have sharp
edges, or who have to be carefully kept.
Generally, by the time you are Real, most

of your hair has been loved off, and your eyes drop out and you get loose in the joints and very shabby. But these things don't matter at all, because once you are Real you can't be ugly, except to people who don't understand."

"I suppose *you* are Real?" said the Rabbit. And then he wished he had not said it, for he thought the Skin Horse might be sensitive. But the Skin Horse only smiled.

"The Boy's Uncle made me Real," he said. "That was a great many years ago; but once you are Real you can't become unreal again. It lasts for always."

The Rabbit sighed. He thought it would be a long time before this magic called Real happened to him. He longed to become Real, to know what it felt like; and yet the idea of growing shabby and losing his eyes and whiskers was rather sad. He wished that he could become it without these uncomfortable things happening to him.

There was a person called Nana who ruled the nursery. Sometimes she took no notice of the playthings lying about, and sometimes, for no reason whatever, she went swooping about like a great wind and hustled them away in cupboards. She called this "tidying up," and the playthings all hated it, especially the tin ones. The Rabbit didn't mind it so much, for wherever he was thrown he came down soft.

One evening, when the Boy was going to bed, he couldn't find the china dog that always slept with him. Nana was in a hurry, and it was too much trouble to hunt for china dogs at bedtime, so she simply looked about her, and seeing that the toy cupboard door stood open, she made a swoop.

"Here," she said, "take your old Bunny! He'll do to sleep with you!" And she dragged the Rabbit

out by one ear and put him into the
Boy's arms.

That night, and for many nights
after, the Velveteen Rabbit slept in the
Boy's bed. At first he found it rather
uncomfortable, for the Boy hugged him
very tight, and sometimes he rolled over
on him, and sometimes he pushed him
so far under the pillow that the Rabbit
could scarcely breathe. And he missed,
too, those long moonlight hours in the
nursery, when all the house was silent,
and his talks with the Skin Horse. But

very soon he grew to like it, for the
Boy used to talk to him, and made nice
tunnels for him under the bedclothes that
he said were like the burrows the real
rabbits lived in. And they had splendid
games together, in whispers, when Nana
had gone away to her supper and left the
nightlight burning on the mantelpiece.
And when the Boy dropped off to sleep,
the Rabbit would snuggle down close
under his little warm chin and dream,
with the Boy's hands clasped close round
him all night long.

And so time went on, and the little
Rabbit was very happy—so happy that he
never noticed how his beautiful velveteen
fur was getting shabbier and shabbier, and
his tail coming unsewn, and all the pink
rubbed off his nose where the Boy had
kissed him.

Spring came, and they had long days
in the garden, for wherever the Boy went
the Rabbit went too. He had rides in the
wheelbarrow, and picnics on the grass,

and lovely fairy huts built for him under the raspberry canes behind the flower border. And once, when the Boy was called away suddenly to go out to tea, the Rabbit was left out on the lawn until long after dusk, and Nana had to come and look for him with the candle because the Boy couldn't go to sleep unless he was there. He was wet through with the dew and quite earthy from diving into the burrows the Boy had made for him in the flower bed, and Nana grumbled as she rubbed him off with a corner of her apron.

"You must have your old Bunny!" she said. "Fancy all that fuss for a toy!"

The Boy sat up in bed and stretched out his hands.

"Give me my Bunny!" he said. "You mustn't say that. He isn't a toy. He's REAL!"

When the little Rabbit heard that, he was happy, for he knew that what the Skin Horse had said was true at last. The nursery magic had happened to him, and he was a toy no longer. He was Real. The Boy himself had said it.

That night he was almost too happy to sleep, and so much love stirred in his little sawdust heart that it almost burst. And into his boot-button eyes, that had long ago lost their polish, there came a look of wisdom and beauty, so that even Nana noticed it next morning when she picked him up and said, "I declare if that old Bunny hasn't got quite a knowing expression!"

That was a wonderful Summer!

Near the house where they lived there was a wood, and in the long June evenings the Boy liked to go there after tea to play. He took the Velveteen Rabbit with him, and before he wandered off to pick flowers, or play at brigands among the trees, he always made the Rabbit a

little nest somewhere among the bracken, where he would be quite cozy, for he was a kind-hearted little boy and he liked Bunny to be comfortable. One evening, while the Rabbit was lying there alone, watching the ants that ran to and fro between his velvet paws in the grass, he saw two strange beings creep out of the tall bracken near him.

They were rabbits like himself, but quite furry and brand-new. They must have been very well made, for their seams didn't show at all, and they changed shape in a queer way when they moved; one minute they were long and thin and the next minute fat and bunchy, instead of always staying the same like he did. Their feet padded softly on the ground, and they crept quite close to him, twitching their noses, while the Rabbit stared hard to see which side the clockwork stuck out, for he knew that people who jump generally have something to wind them up. But he couldn't see it. They were evidently a new kind of rabbit altogether.

They stared at him, and the little Rabbit stared back. And all the time their noses twitched.

"Why don't you get up and play with us?" one of them asked.

"I don't feel like it," said the Rabbit, for he didn't want to explain that he had no clockwork.

"Ho!" said the furry rabbit. "It's as easy as anything." And he gave a big hop sideways and stood on his hind legs.

"I don't believe you can!" he said.

"I can!" said the little Rabbit. "I can jump higher than anything!" He meant when the Boy threw him, but of course he didn't want to say so.

"Can you hop on your hind legs?" asked the furry rabbit.

That was a dreadful question, for the Velveteen Rabbit had no hind legs at all! The back of him was made all in one piece, like a pincushion. He sat still in the bracken and hoped that the other rabbits wouldn't notice.

"I don't want to!" he said again.

But the wild rabbits have very sharp eyes. And this one stretched out his neck and looked.

"He hasn't got any hind legs!" he called out. "Fancy a rabbit without any hind legs!" And he began to laugh.

"I have!" cried the little Rabbit. "I have got hind legs! I am sitting on them!"

"Then stretch them out and show me, like this!" said the wild rabbit. And he began to whirl round and dance, till the little Rabbit got quite dizzy.

"I don't like dancing," he said. "I'd rather sit still!"

But all the while he was longing to dance, for a funny new tickly feeling ran through him, and he felt he would give anything in the world to be able to jump about like these rabbits did.

The strange rabbit stopped dancing and came quite close. He came so close this time that his long whiskers brushed the Velveteen Rabbit's ear, and then he wrinkled his nose suddenly and flattened his ears and jumped backwards.

"He doesn't smell right!" he exclaimed. "He isn't a rabbit at all! He isn't real!"

"I *am* Real!" said the little Rabbit. "I am Real! The Boy said so!" And he nearly began to cry.

Just then there was a sound of footsteps, and the Boy ran past near them, and with a stamp of feet and a flash of white tails the two strange rabbits disappeared.

"Come back and play with me!" called the little Rabbit. "Oh, do come back! I *know* I am Real!"

But there was no answer, only the little ants ran to and fro, and the bracken swayed gently where the two strangers had passed. The Velveteen Rabbit was all alone.

"Oh, dear!" he thought. "Why did they run away like that? Why couldn't they stop and talk to me?"

For a long time he lay very still, watching the bracken, and hoping that they would come back. But they never returned, and presently the sun sank lower and the little white moths fluttered out, and the Boy came and carried him home.

Weeks passed, and the little Rabbit grew very old and shabby, but the Boy loved him just as much. He loved him so hard that he loved all his whiskers off, and the pink lining to his ears turned gray, and his brown spots faded. He even began to lose his shape, and he scarcely looked like a rabbit anymore, except to the Boy. To him he was always beautiful, and that was all that the little Rabbit cared about. He didn't mind how he looked to other people, because the nursery magic had made him Real, and when you are Real shabbiness doesn't matter.

And then, one day, the Boy was ill.

His face grew very flushed, and he talked in his sleep, and his little body was so hot that it burned the Rabbit when he held him close. Strange people came and went in the nursery, and a light burned all night, and through it all the little Velveteen Rabbit lay there, hidden from sight under the bedclothes, and he never stirred, for he was afraid that if they found him someone might take him away, and he knew that the Boy needed him.

It was a long weary time, for the Boy was too ill to play, and the little Rabbit found it rather dull with nothing to do all day long. But he snuggled down patiently, and looked forward to the time when the Boy should be well again, and they would

go out in the garden amongst the flowers
and the butterflies and play splendid
games in the raspberry thicket like they
used to. All sorts of delightful things
he planned, and while the Boy lay half
asleep he crept up close to the pillow and
whispered them in his ear. And presently
the fever turned, and the Boy got better.
He was able to sit up in bed and look
at picture books, while the little Rabbit
cuddled close at his side. And one day,
they let him get up and dress.

It was a bright, sunny morning, and
the windows stood wide open. They had
carried the Boy out onto the balcony,
wrapped in a shawl, and the little Rabbit
lay tangled up among the bedclothes,
thinking.

The Boy was going to the seaside
tomorrow. Everything was arranged,
and now it only remained to carry out
the doctor's orders. They talked about it
all, while the little Rabbit lay under the
bedclothes, with just his head peeping

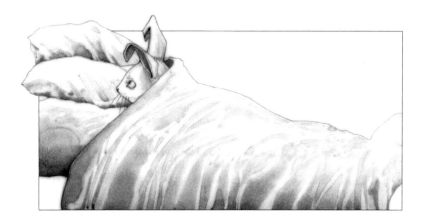

out, and listened. The room was to be disinfected, and all the books and toys that the Boy had played with in bed must be burned.

"Hurrah!" thought the little Rabbit. "Tomorrow we shall go to the seaside!" For the Boy had often talked of the seaside, and he wanted very much to see the big waves coming in, and the tiny crabs, and the sand castles.

Just then Nana caught sight of him.

"How about his old Bunny?" she asked.

"That?" said the doctor. "Why, it's a mass of scarlet fever germs!—Burn it at once. What? Nonsense! Get him a new one. He mustn't have that anymore!"

And so the little Rabbit was put into a sack with the old picture books and a lot of rubbish, and carried out to the end of the garden behind the fowl house. That was a fine place to make a bonfire, only the gardener was too busy just then to attend to it. He had the potatoes to dig and the green peas to gather, but next morning he promised to come quite early and burn the whole lot.

That night the Boy slept in a different bedroom, and he had a new bunny to sleep with him. It was a splendid bunny, all white plush with real glass eyes, but the Boy was too excited to care very much about it. For tomorrow he was going to the seaside, and that in itself was such a wonderful thing that he could think of nothing else.

And while the Boy was asleep, dreaming of the seaside, the little Rabbit lay among the old picture books in the corner behind the fowl house, and he felt very lonely. The sack had been left untied, and so by wriggling a bit he was able to get his head through the opening and look out. He was shivering a little, for he had always been used to sleeping

in a proper bed, and by this time his coat had worn so thin and threadbare from hugging that it was no longer any protection to him. Nearby he could see the thicket of raspberry canes, growing tall and close like a tropical jungle, in whose shadow he had played with the Boy on bygone mornings. He thought of those long sunlit hours in the garden—how happy they were—and a great sadness came over him. He seemed to see them all pass before him, each more beautiful than the other, the fairy huts in the flower bed, the quiet evenings in the wood when he lay in the bracken and the little

ants ran over his paws; the wonderful day
when he first knew that he was Real. He
thought of the Skin Horse, so wise and
gentle, and all that he had told him. Of
what use was it to be loved and lose one's
beauty and become Real if it all ended
like this? And a tear, a real tear, trickled
down his little shabby velvet nose and fell
to the ground.

And then a strange thing happened. For
where the tear had fallen a flower grew
out of the ground, a mysterious
flower, not at all like any that
grew in the garden. It had
slender green leaves the color of
emeralds, and in the center of the
leaves a blossom like a golden
cup. It was so beautiful that the
little Rabbit forgot to cry, and
just lay there watching it. And
presently the blossom opened,
and out of it there stepped a fairy.

She was quite the loveliest
fairy in the whole world. Her

dress was of pearl and dewdrops, and there were flowers round her neck and in her hair, and her face was like the most perfect flower of all. And she came close to the little Rabbit and gathered him up in her arms and kissed him on his velveteen nose that was all damp from crying.

"Little Rabbit," she said, "don't you know who I am?"

The Rabbit looked up at her, and it seemed to him that he had seen her face before, but he couldn't think where.

"I am the nursery magic Fairy," she said. "I take care of all the playthings that the children have loved. When they are old and worn out and the children don't need them anymore, then I come and take them away with me and turn them into Real."

"Wasn't I Real before?" asked the little Rabbit.

"You were Real to the Boy," the Fairy said, "because he loved you. Now you shall be Real to everyone."

And she held the little Rabbit close in her arms and flew with him into the wood.

It was light now, for the moon had risen. All the forest was beautiful, and the fronds of the bracken shone like frosted silver. In the open glade between the tree trunks the wild rabbits danced with their shadows on the velvet grass, but when they saw the Fairy they all stopped dancing and stood round in a ring to stare at her.

"I've brought you a new playfellow," the Fairy said. "You must be very kind to him and teach him all he needs to know in Rabbitland, for he is going to live with you for ever and ever!"

And she kissed the little Rabbit again and put him down on the grass.

"Run and play, little Rabbit!" she said.

But the little Rabbit sat quite still for a moment and never moved. For when he saw all the wild rabbits dancing around him he suddenly remembered about his hind legs, and he didn't want them to see that he was made all in one piece. He

did not know that when the Fairy kissed
him that last time she had changed him
altogether. And he might have sat there
a long time, too shy to move, if just then
something hadn't tickled his nose, and
before he thought what he was doing he
lifted his hind toe to scratch it.

And he found that he actually had hind
legs! Instead of dingy velveteen he had
brown fur, soft and shiny, his ears twitched
by themselves, and his whiskers were so
long that they brushed the grass. He gave
one leap and the joy of using those hind
legs was so great that he went springing
about the turf on them, jumping sideways
and whirling round as the others did, and
he grew so excited that when at last he did
stop to look for the Fairy she had gone.

He was a Real Rabbit at last, at home
with the other rabbits.

Autumn passed and Winter, and in the
Spring, when the days grew warm and
sunny, the Boy went out to play in the

wood behind the house. And while he was playing, two rabbits crept out from the bracken and peeped at him. One of them was brown all over, but the other had strange markings under his fur, as though long ago he had been spotted, and the spots still showed through. And about his little soft nose and his round black eyes there was something familiar, so that the Boy thought to himself:

"Why, he looks just like my old Bunny that was lost when I had scarlet fever!"

But he never knew that it really was his own Bunny, come back to look at the child who had first helped him to be Real.

SHARED INQUIRY BEYOND THE CLASSROOM

The work you have done in Junior Great Books will help you in other school subjects. It will also be useful in parts of your everyday life. In Junior Great Books you have learned to:

Ask questions. This is a good way to learn more about almost anything. Questions help you understand what to do and why to do it, whether you are learning how to bake a cake or ride a skateboard.

Think hard about what things mean. In Junior Great Books, taking your time to really think about a story more than once can help you understand it better. You might see new things you missed the first time. You can do this in your everyday life, too, with art or nature.

Support your ideas with evidence. Sharing your ideas and giving evidence for them are important skills. You will use these skills when you do a project, write a paper, or even ask for more allowance.

Listen to other people's ideas. Hearing what other people say about a story can help you with your own ideas about it. Sometimes you hear something that changes your mind or makes your own idea stronger. Being able to think this way can help you make choices like which sports team to join or how to spend your money.

Respect other points of view. You have seen that people can have different ideas about a story and still be friends. You have also learned how to say politely that you agree or disagree with someone. These things will help you get along with other people in all parts of your life.

GLOSSARY

In this glossary, you will find the meanings of words that are in the Junior Great Books stories you have read. If a word that you are wondering about is not listed here, go to your dictionary for help.

Aa

affectionately: To do something **affectionately** is to do it in a way that shows kindness and love. *After my team lost the game, my father hugged me **affectionately** and said he was still proud of me.*

algae: A life form, found mostly in water, that does not have true roots, stems, or leaves, as plants do. *Seaweed is a type of **algae.***

alley: A narrow path or road that runs behind or between buildings. *Trucks come down the **alley** behind our house to pick up trash.*

Bb

bliss: Great happiness.

boast: To **boast** is to talk about yourself as though you are more important or better than others. *I wish he would not **boast** about his good grades all the time.*

bracken: A kind of fern (a plant with large leaves) or an area where ferns are growing thickly.

brigands: Robbers.

Cc

caught the tone: If you have **caught a tone** from someone, you have picked up that person's way of thinking or speaking about things. *My parents liked that I had **caught the tone** from our polite neighbor and started saying "please" and "thank you" more often.*

current: A **current** of water is a part of a larger body of water that is moving in a certain direction. *We threw leaves in the river and watched the **current** carry them away.*

disinfected / elegant

Dd

disinfected: To **disinfect** something is to clean it in a way that gets rid of any germs. *That cut will need to be **disinfected** right away.*

dreadful: Very bad, or very scary. *The student was sent to the principal's office because of his **dreadful** behavior. Having to spend the night alone in a dark house might be **dreadful** to you.*

drought: A dry time when it doesn't rain. *No plant was left living after the long **drought**.*

Ee

effect: The certain feeling or sense that something gives you. *If you play spooky music on Halloween, the **effect** can be very scary. Painting the walls a light blue color gave the room a calming **effect**.*

elegant: Something or someone **elegant** is beautiful or shows good taste. *The women wore **elegant** dresses to the fancy party.*

eternity: An amount of time that is so long it seems endless. *My parents say I have to wait a year before I can get a new bike, which seems like an **eternity.***

evidently: If something is **evidently** true, it seems to be true because of what you can see or understand. *My father had **evidently** just come home because he was still wearing his work clothes.*

existed: To **exist** is to be living or real. *I wish that unicorns **existed**, but they are make-believe.*

expression: An **expression** is a look on someone's face that shows what that person is thinking or feeling. *I could tell my sister won the race as soon as I saw her happy **expression.***

Ff

fancy: In this story, saying "**fancy**" is a way of showing surprise, like saying "Imagine!" or "Just think!"

feeble: Very weak.

fender: A metal screen placed in front of a fireplace to keep sparks from flying into the room.

Gg

guppies: Small fish often kept as pets.

Ii

insignificant: Not at all important, or having no power. *When my friend lost her backpack she was glad it only had a few insignificant things in it. I felt insignificant in the crowd of older, louder students.*

Jj

jeering: To **jeer** is to make fun of someone or say mean things to someone in a rude way. *Nobody could hear the man give his speech because the crowd was jeering so loudly.*

Ll

lousy: Very bad.

Mm

mechanical: Made or run by machines or machine parts. *The garage has a **mechanical** door that opens when you press a button.*

mockingly: In a mean, teasing way. *Someone who speaks **mockingly** about you might call you nasty names.*

Nn

nix: A way of saying "no."

Oo

obliged: When you are **obliged** to do something, you must do it because you are forced or expected to. *People are **obliged** to stop when a crossing guard holds up his hand. I was **obliged** to be quiet during my baby brother's nap.*

Pp

pity: To feel **pity** is to feel sorry for someone who is in great pain or is unhappy. *We felt pity for the woman whose house burned down.* To **take pity on** someone is to be kind to that person because you feel sorry for him or her. *When my little sister had a bad dream, my parents took pity on her and let her stay in their room.*

plunged: To **plunge** is to dive into something very fast, without fear or without thinking too much about it. *We plunged into the lake, even though we knew how cold it was.*

presently: In a short time. *My brother is out with friends, but he will be home presently.*

professional: Something **professional** is used by (or is good enough to be used by) people who do jobs that need special skills or training. *My father bought some professional pots and pans like the ones restaurant cooks use.* Someone who is a **professional** has the special skills or training to make money doing something that others might do for fun (or no money). *My cousin was so good at baseball that he became a professional player.*

proper: Something **proper** is real and does what it should do. *My parents said I could only go out in the snow if I wore **proper** boots.* Something can also be **proper** if it is right for a certain place or use. *A hammer is the **proper** tool for pounding nails.*

put on airs: If you **put on airs**, you act as if you are more important than others. *The teacher told the fifth-graders not to **put on airs** just because they were the oldest in the school.*

Rr

referring: Calling or drawing attention to something, often by talking about it. *We got tired of the way she kept **referring** to the number of presents she got for her birthday.*

reflecting: When you **reflect** on something, you think about it very carefully. *When my best friend has a birthday, I spend a lot of time **reflecting on** the perfect gift to buy.*

reflection: A **reflection** is the picture you see in a mirror (or something shiny that acts like a mirror). *Looking at the still water of the pond, I could see the **reflection** of the clouds above.*

resign: When you **resign** yourself to something, you give in to it because you know it has to happen no matter what. *I had to resign myself to seeing the dentist because I had a toothache.*

roam: When you **roam**, you move or travel around, often without having a place you are trying to get to. *We decided to roam the town for a while and see what it was like.*

roused: If you **rouse** yourself, you wake up or you start moving. *It is hard to rouse myself to go to early morning soccer practice. The thunderstorm roused my father off the couch to close the window.*

rubbish: Trash.

Ss

scarlet fever: A sickness that gives you a sore throat, fever, and rash.

scourged: To **scourge** is to cause great trouble or unhappiness for something or someone. *People were afraid to leave their homes while the sickness scourged the country.*

sensitive: If you are **sensitive**, you are easily hurt by what other people say or feel about you. *The sensitive boy cried when his friend thought his joke wasn't funny.*

shabby: Something **shabby** looks faded and a little torn up from being used a lot. *I use my school folders every day, and at the end of the year they look shabby.*

sloppy: Messy.

snubbed: To **snub** someone means that you pay no attention to that person or treat him or her without respect. *My friend snubbed me by walking past me in the hall and pretending not to see me.*

splendid: Something **splendid** is very beautiful or excellent. *A male peacock has splendid tail feathers. The crowd stood up and cheered at the end of the splendid play.*

stereo: A machine (or group of machines) that plays music through two speakers. *A stereo often has a radio and a CD player.*

submerged: Something that is **submerged** is all the way under water. *The sandcastle was submerged when the tide rose up onto the beach.*

succession: A number of things or people that follow each other in order. *My brother has lost a succession of baseball games this summer.*

superior: Better or finer than other people or things. *Fresh fish from the ocean is superior to the kind you buy in a can.* When people act **superior**, they act as if they are better than everyone else. *At the restaurant, he ordered the waiter around in a superior way.*

swagger: To **swagger** is to walk in a bold, proud way. *You might swagger across the field after your team wins a soccer game.*

swooping, swoop: To **swoop** is to rush in or down quickly. *We watched the owls swooping down from the trees to catch their food.*

Tt

tourniquet: A cord or a tight bandage used to stop the flow of blood to a part of the body. *The nurse put a tourniquet around my arm to stop it from bleeding.*

Vv

VCR: Short for "video cassette recorder," a machine that connects to a television and records shows

Yy

yore: Yore means a long time ago and is usually used with "of" in the phrase, "of yore." *In days of **yore**, knights and ladies lived in castles.*

ACKNOWLEDGMENTS

All possible care has been taken to trace ownership and secure permission for each selection in this series. The Great Books Foundation wishes to thank the following authors, publishers, and representatives for permission to reproduce copyrighted materials:

The Wise Little Toad, from LA SAPITA SABIA Y OTROS CUENTOS, by Rosario Ferré. Copyright © 1997 by Rosario Ferré. Published by Alfaguara, Mexico. Reproduced by permission of Susan Bergholz Literary Services. English translation by Helen Lane. Translation © 2002 by The Great Books Foundation.

DOODLE FLUTE, by Daniel Pinkwater. Copyright © 1991 by Daniel Pinkwater. Published by Macmillan Publishing Company. Reproduced by permission of the author.

ILLUSTRATION CREDITS

Illustrations for *The Wise Little Toad* copyright © 2014 by Rich Lo.

Illustrations for *Doodle Flute* copyright © 1991 by Daniel Pinkwater. Reproduced by permission of the author.

Illustrations for *The Velveteen Rabbit* copyright ©1992 by Donna Diamond.

Cover art copyright © 2014 by Jose Ramirez.

Design by THINK Book Works.